Dr. Bird to the Rescue

A TALE FROM THE DESERT

Story by D.J. Smith
Illustrations by Kevin Kibsey

ARIZONA HIGHWAYS
BOOKS

The desert is a strange place where summers

Yet, lots of plants and animals live there,
including many types of cactus.

2

are very, very hot.

3

A cactus is a

4

strange kind of plant.

It doesn't need much water, and it has flowers but no leaves.
Instead of leaves, a cactus has sharp needles.

Sammy is a saguaro (suh-WAR-oh) cactus.
He lives in the Sonoran Desert, the only place in the
whole world that saguaros call home.
Sammy's home is near Tucson, in a special place
called the Saguaro National Park, which helps
kids and adults learn all about the desert.

Saguaros are the giants of the desert.

They can live to be 200 years old and weigh more than a big truck.

In saguaro years, Sammy's a teenager.

If he stays healthy, he could grow to be as tall as a five-story building.

Today, Sammy is sick.
A cactus gets sick, just like people do.
He wants to get well, so

Sammy tries asking his neighbors for help. 7

First, a big Gila (He-la) monster comes strolling by.
He looks mean and grouchy.

"Excuse me, please," says Sammy. "I'm sick. Can you help me?"

Shaking his blunt head, the Gil

monster hisses, "S-s-s-sorry.

We're different.
I'm a reptile;
you're a plant.
Adios-s-s-s, amigo."

9

Next, a brown and white cactus wren flies around

10

Sammy, inspecting him up and down.

Landing on his arm, she says in a scratchy voice, "You're looking a little run down."

"It's true," replies Sammy, "I'm feeling poorly. Can you help me?"

"Not me!" says the busy bird. "You're too different. You're a plant; you don't even have feathers. Besides, I have to get going. I'm trying to find a decent place to live!"

She flutters away.

11

A hungry lizard starts
to climb up Sammy's
side, tickling
his ribs.

"I say, have you seen any bugs?" asks the lizard.

"Not lately," answers
Sammy. "But maybe you
can help me. I'm
feeling rotten."

"Dear, dear. I'm terribly sorry, sport,
but since you're a plant and I'm a reptile,
there's really nothing I can do for you.
Now, I absolutely *must* find something to eat.
Ta, ta!"

Finally, a tiny elf owl peeks out of a hole in a big cactus next to Sammy.

The sick saguaro moans, "I feel terrible, but no one will help me."

After circling around Sammy and looking at him closely, the elf owl chirps, "Sammy, there's a big, oozy spot near your top; it looks like an infection.

I think you need to see the doctor."

"But," says Sammy. "How can I do that?
I'm a plant; I can't move around like
birds and animals do."

"No problem," says the wise little owl. "The doctor ca

As the owl flies off to call the doctor,
Sammy begins to feel better.
Someone's finally trying to help him.

ome to you."

17

Soon, a colorful bird with a pointy beak lands
on Sammy's arm. His eyes are bright and shiny.
Black and white bars cover his wings and back.
He wears a cap of bright red feathers on his head.

"Did a little owl send you?" asks Sammy.

"Yes. I'm Dr. Bird and I'm here to help you."

"I've seen you before," Sammy says.
Aren't you a woodpecker?"

"Yes, I'm a Gila woodpecker," Dr. Bird replies
as he examines Sammy.

"I see your problem, Sammy.

Some bugs are attacking you.
After I clean them out, you'll be fine."

"Will it hurt?" asks Sammy.

"Not at all." And using his very sharp beak,
he begins to peck away at the bugs.

21

"Yummy, yummy

22

hese bugs are tasty!"

Soon, there's a nice, clean hole.
Sammy's sore spot is all gone.

"You should feel better now."

"I sure do," sighs Sammy. "Thank you. You helped me
when no one else would, even though we're different."

"Our differences don't really matter, you know," says the bird.

"We're all part of Nature's community. We nee

"I know you've helped me. But how can I help others?" asks Sammy.

"You already do many good things," declares the smart bird.

"Really?" asks Sammy. "Like what?"

24

to help each other."

25

"You produce fruit for me and other creatures to eat.

And your blossoms
attract bugs that are also
food. Even the hole in your
side is helpful. It makes a safe
place to build a nest."

27

"Wow! you're right, Dr. Bird.
Being helpful makes me happy."

"Me, too," says the satisfied woodpecker.

Then, Dr. Bird salutes Sammy and soars away.

29

"That looks a lot like . . ."

You're right! Illustrator Kevin Kibsey's fanciful, yet amazingly accurate, watercolors showcase the Sonoran Desert's diversity. If you look closely, you'll see some of his favorite critters and landmarks: *[Underlining indicates that there's a photograph of the creature on the opposite page.]*

MATURE SAGUARO
A saguaro begins branching when it is about 60 years old, producing arms where its trunk is thickest.

CACTUS WREN
The cactus wren, the state bird of Arizona, builds a neat grass nest, often locating it in a cavity (called a "boot") in a saguaro cactus.

GILA WOODPECKER
Although Gila woodpeckers feed mainly on insects, these noisy natives of the saguaro forests also dine on dates, pomegranates, and nuts.

TOM VEZO

ELF OWL
Elf owls, among the smallest owls in the world, spend their summers in southern Arizona, where they like to build nests in saguaros or sycamore trees.

... And how they really look ...

YOUNG SAGUARO
Tender seedlings and infant saguaros need protection from strong sunlight in order to grow. Rocks and trees like the paloverde provide shade for a cactus when it is young.

GILA MONSTER
Slow-moving and venomous, Gila monsters are the largest lizards in the United States. They prefer to spend most of their time underground.

COLLARED LIZARD
When it needs to move at high speed, the collared lizard stands upright and runs on its rear legs. If trapped, it will bite.

Designer **MARY WINKELMAN VELGOS**
Book Editors **BOB ALBANO** AND **PK PERKIN McMAHON**
Photography **MARTY CORDANO** (EXCEPT PHOTOS OF AUTHOR, ILLUSTRATOR, AND ELF OWL)
Premedia and Color Imaging **AMERICAN COLOR**

Printed in Hong Kong.
Library of Congress Catalog Number 2004117533
ISBN 1-932082-08-5

Published by the Book Division of *Arizona Highways*® magazine, a monthly publication of the Arizona Department
of Transportation, 2039 West Lewis Avenue, Phoenix, Arizona 85009.
Telephone: (602) 712-2200

Web site: www.arizonahighways.com

Publisher: Win Holden
Managing Editor: Bob Albano
Associate Editor: Evelyn Howell
Associate Editor: PK Perkin McMahon
Director of Photography: Peter Ensenberger
Production Director: Kim Ensenberger
Production Assistants: Annette Phares, Vicky Snow